S0-BAV-270

Lilly to the Rescue

Brenda Bellingham

Lilly to the Rescue

Illustrations by Kathy Kaulbach

FIRST NOVELS

The New Series

Formac Publishing Limited
Halifax, Nova Scotia

Formac Publishing Company Limited acknowledges the support of The Canada Council and the Nova Scotia Department of Education and Culture in the development of writing and publishing in Canada.

Canadian Cataloguing in Publication Data

Bellingham, Brenda, 1931-

   Lilly to the rescue

   (First novel series)

ISBN 0-88780-386-5 (pbk)   ISBN 0-88780-387-3 (bound)

I. Kaulbach, Kathy R. (Kathy Rose), 1955- II. Title. III. Series.

PS8553.E468L55 1997   jC813'.54   C96-950186-2
PZ7.B414Li 1997

Formac Publishing Limited
5502 Atlantic Street
Halifax, NS B3H 1G4

Printed and bound in Canada.

Contents

1
Wanted: Best Friend

I wished my family would hurry through breakfast. I wanted to walk to school with Minna, and she always left early. Macdonald didn't want to hurry. He yelled and thumped his feet against his highchair.

"What's wrong, Mac?" Mom groaned. "Eat your cereal." She was trying to use her curling iron and drink her coffee at the same time.

"He doesn't want *Chew-Chews*," I said. "He wants *O-O-Oh So Goods*!" I put Mac's bowl of *Chew-Chews* in front of

Pop. He's my step-father and his name is Peter Otis Pond. That's why I call him Pop. I poured *O-O-Oh So Goods*! for Macdonald. He crammed a fistful into his mouth.

"I wish he'd try to talk," Mom said. Macdonald's two years old.

"Why should he?" Pop said, gulping down *Chew-Chews*. "Lilly talks for him. He'd talk if we made him ask for what he wants."

"No, he wouldn't," I cried. "He'd starve to death. How could you treat your own son that way?" Macdonald's only my half brother, but I love him like a whole one.

Pop put up his hands in surrender. "Sorry, Tiger! It was just a thought."

"Look at the time!" Mom grabbed Macdonald and her purse.

Pop grabbed the baby-bag and his briefcase. Everybody kissed everybody else. Mac tasted like *O-O-Oh So Goods*!

"Bye, Big Mac," I said. "Have a good time at day-care." He clung to my neck. That's the trouble with good-bye kisses. They make you feel homesick for people. Hello kisses are the best kind.

After my family left, I had to clean the kitchen. First I loaded the dishwasher. Next I wiped up the gooey stuff on Mac's high-chair. Yuk!

Through the kitchen window I saw Barb Kristoff and Delaney Boychuk walking to school.

They'd go a few steps, then stop. Barb said something and Delaney doubled up laughing. They were telling secrets. Best friends do that.

It was like looking through a fish bowl. I was the fish. Never keep only one fish in a bowl. Even a fish needs a best friend. I used to have a best friend, but she moved away. We both cried. Her mother told her not to be silly. "It's time you learned to stand on your own two feet," she said. I thought it was a dumb thing to say. Since then I haven't had a best friend.

At last I finished my chores and I could call for Minna. She wasn't my best friend yet, but I really wished she would be.

2
I Deal with Theresa

Minna's grandma looks after her while her parents work. She said Minna had already left.

I found Minna dodging from tree to tree. One of our neighbours down the street has a dog named Superdog—"Soup" for short. He barks like crazy when people pass his yard. Minna is a bit scared of things like dogs, but she's brave in other ways. For one thing, she plays piano in the music festival—in front of judges. I'd die.

"Don't worry about Soup," I said. "He's fenced in."

"I'm not worried," she said, tossing her long, black hair over her shoulder.

I wished I could do that. Pop says I'm lucky to be tall and strong. I'd rather be small and pretty, like Minna. She was born here, but her family came from China.

"What's wrong then?" I asked. "Are you being chased by aliens?"

"No," she said, giggling, "tree-monsters."

Minna's giggle is catching. The two of us giggled 'til our bellies ached.

"Let's run or we'll be late," she said at last.

We caught up to Kendall. His family just moved into the house next to Minna's. None of

us noticed Theresa Green. She ran up behind and pushed Minna hard in the back.

"Minnie Mouse!" Theresa yelled, and ran off laughing.

Minna's head jerked backwards. I could tell she wanted to cry, but she didn't.

"I hate that girl," Kendall said. "I think she pushes me because I'm new, and she pushes Minna because Minna is small and looks different."

I raced after Theresa and cornered her against the school wall. I was *so* mad. I thought I'd burst and blood-red anger would pour out.

"If you do that again," I shouted, "I'll push you so hard your head will fall off!" I glared my fiercest glare—number ten on the tiger scale. When she started to sniff and rub her eyes, I let her go.

"Minna should tell the principal," Kendall said.

"No, she shouldn't," I said. "Theresa will call her a crybaby. If she pushes you or Minna again, I'll deal with her."

Kendall's face got red. "Wanna bet?" he said. "You're not the boss around here. I can look after myself."

"I don't want her to hurt you," Minna said.

I ignored Kendall. I didn't even give him one of my tiger glares. Minna cared about me! Cool!

3
My Favourite Day

After school, Kendall and Minna waited for me. Theresa was in the playground, hanging upside down from the monkey bars.

"Want to walk home with us?" Kendall asked me.

He seemed to have forgotten he could look after himself. I almost told him to get lost, but Minna was chewing the ends of her hair. I'd promised to look after Minna and Kendall, and what kind of friend breaks a promise?

"Okay," I said.

Theresa stayed where she

belonged—on the monkey bars.

"Friday is my favourite day," I said on the way home. "What are you going to do this weekend?"

"Build a tree-fort," Kendall said.

"Great idea!" I said. "I'll help. You can help, too, Minna." She didn't come out to play much. You can't get to be best friends with someone unless you see her all the time.

Minna's eyes smiled. "I've always wanted a tree-house," she said.

"Not a tree-house, a tree-fort," Kendall said.

"Pop's got some wood we can use," I said.

Kendall and Minna went home to change their clothes.

By the time they came over, I had dragged some wood out of our garage.

"First we have to nail a couple of two-by-fours across the branches," I said.

"How do *you* know?" Kendall asked.

"Pop told me," I said. "I started to build a tree-fort once, but I changed my mind." I swung myself up into the tree. "Pass the wood up. I'll start nailing."

"No," Kendall said. "Bring it to my yard."

"Your trees are only teen-agers, Kendall," I said. "We've got an adult tree. It doesn't matter whose yard it's in. You can play in our yard any time you like. You too, Minna."

Kendall's neck got red all the way around to the back. "I'm going home," he said, and he stomped off.

"He sure argues a lot," I said to Minna. "What's he so mad about? I was only trying to help."

I bet Barb would tell Delaney that Kendall was a dumb jerk. A best friend is always on your side.

Minna wriggled as if she needed the bathroom. "I think he wants to be in charge," she said.

"He doesn't know how to build a tree-fort," I said. "And he'd break his dad's tree. His dad would be wild."

"I guess so," Minna said. She handed me a piece of wood and

I nailed it. A few minutes later, she said she had to go home for supper.

"Come over tomorrow," I said. Somehow, I knew she wouldn't. Forget what I said about Friday being my favourite day. I hate Fridays.

4
Minna Gets Mad

On Monday morning I called for Minna. Maybe she was too shy to come over on her own. I didn't bother about Kendall.

"I'm not going to school today," Minna said. "I'm sick."

"No, you're not," I said. "You're scared."

"Being scared makes you sick," Minna said.

That was true. "You don't have to be scared of Theresa Green," I said. "I'll walk with you."

Minna hesitated. She was chewing her hair again.

"Your parents will be mad if

you don't go to school," I said.

"I know." She sighed. "I'll get my jacket."

The closer we got to school, the slower Minna walked. If her hair wasn't so long she'd have eaten it all.

Usually I don't hold Pop's hand. I'm too old. But when I do, his hand is big and warm and makes me feel safe. "Hold my hand," I said to Minna.

She snatched her hand away. "I know I'm small, but I'm not a baby," she yelled. She was spitting mad like a little cat.

I got pretty mad myself. I forgot I wanted to be best friends with her.

"Well, excuse me," I said. "I was only trying to make you feel better."

When you try to help someone you like and she screams at
you, you feel all mixed up. Sad
and angry whirl around together.

I walked behind Minna. If
only Theresa would show up,
that would show Minna. I'd
rescue her. Afterwards she'd
fall, sobbing, at my feet and beg

me to forgive her. Where was Theresa when I needed her?

On the other side of the street, that's where. When she saw me look, she crossed her eyes, stretched her mouth with her little fingers, and stuck out her tongue. She looked even worse than usual, but she wasn't pushing anyone. I hoped Minna would notice. I think she did.

"I'm sorry I yelled at you, Lilly," she said, when we got to school. "It's just … well, I hate being small."

I tried to stay mad, but I couldn't. "That's okay," I said. "I hate being big."

5
Bossy-boots

A few days later, our room went on a field trip to the Pioneer Farm. I found a good seat on the bus. Minna sat beside me. I didn't even have to ask her. On the way there we had a sing-a-long. I sang louder than anybody. That's how I felt. At the farm the other kids hung back.

"Try to keep up," the guide said.

"Come on, you guys," I said. I didn't want him to think no one liked him, so I walked beside him. Our teacher, Miss

Riley, came behind to make sure no one got lost.

Our last stop was the barn. The cows came plodding in from the field to be milked.

"Who told them it was time?" Kendall asked.

"Bossy did." The guide patted Bossy's shoulder as she went by. "In every herd you'll find a boss cow. Right, Bossy?" Bossy mooed.

"How does a cow get to be boss?" Theresa asked.

I bet she wanted to take lessons.

"She beats up on the others," said Monty. He always draws pictures of guns and bombs.

"Sometimes cows fight," our guide said. "Often they just seem to agree who is boss."

"Time to go," Miss Riley said. "The buses are here." The cows munched hay while they were being milked. The air smelled like flowers. I didn't feel like moving.

"What's keeping everybody?" Miss Riley asked.

"We're waiting for Lilly," Kendall said. "She always goes first." He grinned up at our guide. "Like Bossy."

"Bossy-boots," Theresa chanted, smirking at me.

I didn't care what Theresa said. She wanted to get back at me. But the other kids giggled. Even Minna smiled. I tried to give Theresa one of my tiger glares. It fizzled out. Maybe it was because my eyes were wet.

"Get going," Miss Riley said.

I went last. On the bus I sat beside Minna, but I didn't sing. You can't sing when your heart feels bruised and your throat has a big lump in it. Minna thought I was a bossy-boots. She'd never want to be my best friend.

6
Face It

On Saturday Kendall hauled Minna over to his place to help with his fort. I could see them from my bedroom window. Finally he broke a tree branch. His dad jumped around, waving his arms and yelling. I should have felt glad, but I didn't.

"Want to come shopping with us?" Mom asked. "We're taking Macdonald."

"No, thanks," I said. "Shopping is boring."

So was playing on my own.

Face it, I told myself. *Either you can die of boredom, or prove to Minna and Kendall you aren't a bossy-boots.* I decided I'd rather live. But how could I get them to give me another chance? They were cleaning up the yard. I bet they were bored too.

I scrabbled through my closet and found a cape and sword from Hallowe'en. With an old satchel slung across my body I looked like one of the three musketeers. Then I dodged down the back lane to Kendall's yard. On the way I called out to some imaginary people. Kendall and Minna looked over Kendall's back fence.

"What are you doing?" Kendall asked.

"Looking for adventures," I said. "All's quiet at the fort. The

captain sent us out to scout around. Want to come with us?"

"I don't see anybody," Kendall said, frowning. "Only you."

"The other guys were eaten by a man-eating crocodile," I said.

"A man-eating crocodile!" Kendall said. "Wait a minute. I'll get my sword."

7
Superdog

"See you," Minna said.

"Wait!" I cried. "Don't you want to be a scout?"

"Not really," Minna said.

Oh no! If she wouldn't play, she'd never find out I'd changed.

"Listen," I said. "I've just remembered. The captain said some people can go along to watch. They can write up the adventures afterwards."

Minna loves writing stories. Our teacher always reads them out because Minna doesn't read loud enough. She's only loud on the piano.

Her eyes got all shiny. "Okay," she said. "I'll be the reporter. But I don't want to fight."

"I'll do the fighting," Kendall said. He came out of his house wearing a red sweatsuit, a shirt made out of fish net, and a shiny plastic helmet with wires sticking out of the top. "I'm a Viking," he said.

He looked more like a lobster.

"This is my trusty sword, Thor," he said, waving a plastic sword. "What do we do first?"

"What do you want to do?" I asked, remembering not to be bossy.

"Search for buried treasure," Kendall said. "It's on an island in the Amazon. The jungle is full of snakes and crocodiles

and panthers and things."

A Viking in the jungle? Weird!

"Follow me," Kendall said.

"I don't think we're supposed to play in the back lane," Minna said, "because of cars."

I knew that, but I didn't dare say anything. Not being bossy is very hard to do.

"Let's say the middle of the lane is the Amazon," Kendall said. "We'll keep to the banks to avoid enemy war canoes."

There weren't any war canoes. Most people were away doing Saturday things, or mowing their front yards.

Kendall got to go first. Minna came last because she wanted to. Kendall whacked at the weeds and tall grass. Once in a

while he whacked a garbage can. Maybe he was trying to scare the wild animals. He sure scared Superdog.

8
Bossy-boots Again

Superdog stood on his hind legs and scrabbled at the fence.

"A wild animal!" Kendall yelled. "I'll protect you." He poked his plastic sword through the narrow gap between the boards.

The point pricked Superdog in the chest. It didn't really hurt him, but it made him mad. He tried to scramble over the fence so that he could eat Kendall. I didn't blame him. Kendall growled back at Superdog.

"Please, Kendall, stop," Minna pleaded. "He'll bite you."

"No way!" Kendall cried. "Come on, alligator, come and get me." Then he did a really dumb thing. He stood on the garbage can box and waved his sword over the fence.

Superdog backed away. He pulled back his lips and showed us his huge teeth. The fur on his neck stood up. Soup has long legs. If he leaped high enough he'd get Kendall's nose. Kendall was dumb, but he didn't deserve to lose his nose.

Kendall laughed. Superdog kicked up the ground with his back feet. If he jumped the fence, he'd tear Kendall to pieces. Kendall would look like a piece of raw beef that someone lost in the lane. There'd be blood running out of him. I felt sick. Besides, people would blame Soup and it wasn't his fault.

I forgot not to be bossy. I grabbed Kendall by the back of his shirt. He held on to the top of the fence. I yanked as hard as I could. Kendall lost his grip and staggered backwards. His shirt ripped. As it gave way, I lost my

balance. I thought a pickup truck had dropped on me. It was Kendall. He should go on a diet.

9
Best Friends

Kendall scrambled up and glared at me. "Now look what you did!" he yelled. "You ripped my shirt."

"It's your own fault," Minna said. "It's mean to tease a dog. Dangerous too. And you hurt Lilly."

She sounded as mad as the day I tried to hold her hand.

I couldn't believe my ears. Neither could Kendall.

"I'm sorry," he said. "I didn't mean to fall on you."

"I'm sorry about your shirt," I gasped. I was still short of breath from when Kendall landed on me.

"My mom made it," Kendall said. "It's the only one in existence."

"If you like, I'll ask my grandma to mend it," Minna said. "She's very good at sewing."

"That would be great." Kendall cheered up. He sniffed. "I smell hamburgers."

He was lucky he still had a nose to smell with.

"I hit my head on a rock," I said.

"And I got a dent in my Viking helmet," Kendall said. "You should've left me alone, Lilly. I've told you. I can look after myself. I'm hungry. I'm going home."

Sometimes you can't pretend you don't care, no matter how much you want to. My eyes filled with tears, and I had to wipe my nose on my shirt. "Nobody likes me," I moaned.

Minna sat beside me in the dirt. "I like you," she said.

"How can you?" I said. "I'm such a bossy-boots."

"There is an old Chinese saying," Minna said. "To save foolish person, wise person must sometimes be bossy."

"Really?" I said. "It doesn't sound very Chinese."

She grinned.

"You're teasing," I said. Usually Minna doesn't say anything about being Chinese. She really must like me. Suddenly I felt light and fluttery, like a bird. I

got up and staggered around. My legs wouldn't go where I wanted them to. "I feel woozy," I said.

"Would you like to lean on me?" Minna asked.

"Yes, please," I said. I put my arm around her shoulders and she put her arm around my waist. We walked home together—like really, truly best friends. I almost started to cry again. It's weird how being happy can make you do that.

10
Mind Reader

"Where have you been?" Mom demanded.

Pop frowned. "Have you been fighting?" he asked.

In a way I had. My head was still throbbing and before I could think what to say, Minna answered.

"Lilly saved Kendall's life," she said. "He was almost killed by a mad dog."

The way she threw back her long, black hair, you could tell she thought my parents didn't appreciate me. Their mouths fell open.

"I have to go home now," Minna said. "My grandma will be looking for me. I hope your head feels better soon, Lilly. I'll come over and see you tomorrow, okay?"

After Minna left, I told Mom and Pop what had really happened. They said they were proud of me. Pop took me to the doctor about the lump on my head.

The doctor made some dumb jokes, but he said I'd be okay. "You're a smart girl," he said.

On the way back to the car I held Pop's hand. "Today it was okay to be bossy," I said. "Mostly it isn't. How come?"

Pop scratched his head. "That's a tough one, Tiger. Sometimes people *really* need help, and sometimes they don't.

As you get older you'll learn the difference."

"Man," I said. "Now I have to be a mind reader. This isn't going to be easy."

Next day, Minna came over. Macdonald was trying to hitch a toy wagon to his toy tractor. He looked as if he needed some help, but maybe he didn't. How was I to know?

Minna knelt down in front of him. "Macdonald, can we help?" she asked.

Mac held up his toys and beamed at me. "Lilly do."

"Hey, Macdonald can talk!" I yelled.

"He loves you, Lilly," Minna said. "I'll tell you a secret. I wish I had a little brother. It's not much fun being an only child."

"You can share Macdonald," I said.

"We can pretend we're sisters," Minna said.

We looked in the mirror and we both began to giggle. Minna is the best best-friend in the whole world.

Meet five other great kids in the New First Novels Series:

- ## Meet Morgan the Magician
  ### in *Morgan Makes Magic*
  by Ted Staunton/Illustrated by Bill Slavin

  When he's in a tight spot, Morgan tells stories — and most of them stretch the truth, to say the least. But when he tells kids at his new school he can do magic tricks, he really gets in trouble — most of all with the dreaded Aldeen Hummel!

- ## Meet Jan the Curious
  ### in *Jan's Big Bang*
  by Monica Hughes/Illustrated by Carlos Friere

  Taking part in the Science Fair is a big deal for Grade Three kids, but Jan and her best friend Sarah are ready for the challenge. Still, finding a safe project isn't easy, and the girls discover that getting ready for the fair can cause a whole lot of trouble.

- ## Meet Robyn the Dreamer
  ### in *Shoot for the Moon, Robyn*
  by Hazel Hutchins/ Illustrated by Yvonne Cathcart

  When the teacher asks her to sing for the class, Robyn knows it's her chance to be the world's best singer. Should she perform like Celine Dion, or do *My Bonnie Lies Over the Ocean*, or the matchmaker song? It's hard to decide, even for the world's best singer — and the three boys who throw spitballs don't make it any easier.

• Meet Duff the Daring
in *Duff the Giant Killer*
by Budge Wilson/Illustrated by Kim LaFave
Getting over the chicken pox can be boring, but Duff and Simon find a great way to enjoy themselves — acting out one of their favourite stories, *Jack the Giant Killer*, in the park. In fact, they do it so well the police get into the act.

• Meet Carrie the Courageous
in *Go For It, Carrie*
by Lesley Choyce/ Illustrated by Mark Thurman
More than anything else, Carrie wants to roller-blade. Her big brother and his friend just laugh at her. But Carrie knows she can do it if she just keeps trying. As her friend Gregory tells her, "You can do it, Carrie. Go for it!"

Look for these First Novels!

- *About Arthur*
  Arthur Throws a Tantrum
  Arthur's Dad
  Arthur's Problem Puppy

- *About Fred*
  Fred and the Stinky Cheese
  Fred's Dream Cat

- *About the Loonies*
  Loonie Summer
  The Loonies Arrive

- *About Maddie*
  Maddie in Hospital
  Maddie Goes to Paris
  Maddie in Danger
  Maddie in Goal
  Maddie Wants Music
  That's Enough Maddie!

- *About Mikey*
  Good For You, Mikey Mite!
  Mikey Mite Goes to School
  Mikey Mite's Big Problem

- *About Mooch*
  Mooch Forever
  Hang On, Mooch!
  Mooch Gets Jealous
  Mooch and Me

- *About the Swank Twins*
  The Swank Prank
  Swank Talk

- *About Max*
  Max the Superhero

Formac Publishing Company Limited
5502 Atlantic Street, Halifax, Nova Scotia B3H 1G4
Orders: 1-800-565-1975 Fax: (902) 425-0166